THE GIFT OF CHRISTMAS

NORTH-SOUTH BOOKS / NEW YORK / LONDON

The Gift of Christmas

By **Philemon Sturges**

Illustrated by **Holly Berry**

A dark green pine
Bedecked with bright

Colored balls and sparkling light;
An angel, Santa, popcorn chains,
Toys, trinkets, tinsel, candy canes!

The sights of Christmas!
Oh, can there be
Anything so grand to see?

A sleigh bell in the silent night?
The stocking's filled! Cries of delight!
Crisp papers rip, a ribbon snaps,
We all sing carols, Grandma claps!

Hark! Hark!
It's Christmas!
To every ear,
Christmas sounds
Are good to hear.

Cinnamon and baking dough,
Fresh-cut fir with mistletoe,
Scented candles, smoke from the fire;
Wet wool mittens getting drier.

The smells of Christmas!
An old dog knows —
At Christmas
One must have a nose!

Roast stuffed turkey? No, a goose!
Sweet plum pudding, chocolate mousse,
Sticky dates, vanilla creams,
Apples, quinces, tangerines!

The tastes of Christmas!
So rich and sweet.
On Christmas day
We eat and eat!

The crisp air chills
A tingling nose,

Hot chocolate warms us to our toes.
A grizzled cheek, as rough as sand,
Soft silken hair, a child's warm hand.

The feel of Christmas!
The warmth, the cold –
There is so much
To touch and hold.

Bright Christmas sights, glad sounds, and such
Sweet smells, rich tastes, soft things to touch.
And yet what sets our hearts ablaze?
A newborn infant's wondrous gaze!

The gift of Christmas!
The great joy of
A heart that's filled
With hope and love.

To Philemon and Ros, who gave me my life
and filled it with hope and love. —P.S.

To Judy Sue and Philemon. —H.B.

Published in the United States by North-South Books Inc., New York.
Published simultaneously in Great Britain, Canada, Australia, and
New Zealand in 1995 by North-South Books, an imprint of
Nord-Süd Verlag AG, Gossau Zürich, Switzerland.

Library of Congress Cataloging-in-Publication Data
Sturges, Philemon.
The Gift of Christmas / by Philemon Sturges ; illustrated by Holly Berry.
Summary: Christmas brings bright sights, glad sounds, rich tastes,
and other good things, but the newborn infant brings the greatest joy.
[1. Christmas—Fiction. 2. Stories in rhyme.] I. Berry, Holly, ill. II. Title.
PZ8.3.S922Jo 1995
[e]—dc20 95-1644

A CIP catalogue record for this book is available from The British Library.

ISBN 1-55858-469-2 (TRADE BINDING)
1 3 5 7 9 TB 10 8 6 4 2
ISBN 1-55858-470-6 (LIBRARY BINDING)
1 3 5 7 9 LB 10 8 6 4 2
Calligraphy by Colleen
Printed in Belgium